W9-BGI-297

A NOTE TO PARENTS

Disney's First Readers Level 3 books were developed for children who have mastered many basic reading skills and are on the road to becoming competent and confident readers.

Disney's First Readers Level 3 books have more fully developed plots, introduce harder words, and use more complex sentence and paragraph structures than Level 2 books.

Reading is the single most important way a young person learns to enjoy reading. Give your child opportunities to read many different types of literature. Make books, magazines, and writing materials available to your child. Books that are of special interest to your child will motivate more reading and provide more enjoyment. Here are some additional tips to help you spend quality reading time with your child:

★ Promote thinking skills. Ask if your child liked the story or not and why. This is one of the best ways to learn if your child understood what he or she has read.

★ Continue to read aloud. No matter how old the child may be, or how proficient a reader, hearing a delightful story read aloud is still exciting and a very important part of becoming a more fluent reader.

★ Read together on a regular basis, and encourage your child to read to you often. Be a good teacher by being a good listener and audience!

★ Praise all reading efforts, no matter how small.

★ Try out the After-Reading Fun activities at the end of each book to enhance the skills your child has already learned.

Remember that early-reading experiences that you share with your child can help him or her to become a confident and successful reader later on!

— Patricia Koppman
Past President
International Reading Association

Designed by Disney Global Design Group

Copyright © 2002 Disney Enterprises, Inc.
All rights reserved.

No part of this publication may be reproduced in whole or in part,
or stored in a retrieval system, or transmitted in any form or by any means,
electronic, mechanical, photocopying, recording, or otherwise,
without written permission of the copyright holder.
For information regarding permission, write to:
Disney Licensed Publishing,
114 Fifth Avenue, New York, New York 10011

First published by Random House, Inc., New York, New York.
This edition published by Scholastic Inc.,
90 Old Sherman Turnpike, Danbury, Connecticut 06816
by arrangement with Disney Licensed Publishing.

SCHOLASTIC and associated logos are trademarks of Scholastic Inc.

ISBN 0-7172-6659-1

Printed in the U.S.A.

Go, Stitch, Go!

by Monica Kulling
Illustrated by Denise Shimabukuro and
the Disney Storybook Artists

Disney's First Readers — Level 3
A Story from Disney's *Lilo & Stitch*

SCHOLASTIC INC.
New York   Toronto   London   Auckland   Sydney
Mexico City   New Delhi   Hong Kong   Buenos Aires

One afternoon, Lilo saw Myrtle riding her trike up the street.

"Hey, Myrtle!" Lilo yelled with a wave. She really wanted to be Myrtle's friend. "I got a new dog!" Lilo said. "His name is Stitch."

But Myrtle didn't like Lilo. She thought Lilo was weird.

"Ewwww!" said Myrtle. "That is the ugliest dog I ever saw."

Stitch made a face and stuck out his tongue. He thought the same thing about Myrtle!

Actually, Stitch was not a dog at all. Stitch was really an alien who had crash-landed in Hawaii! He had tried to make himself look like a dog—sort of—so that Lilo would pick him at the animal rescue center. So far, his plan had worked!

But two other aliens named Jumba and Pleakley wanted to capture Stitch. They tried to dress as tourists. And Pleakley even had to pretend he was a woman!

Pleakley was an expert about Earth. "We have to blend in," he reminded Jumba.

But then Pleakley tripped over Jumba's foot. "Whoa!" he yelled as his wig went flying!

That did it! Stitch saw Pleakley—
and then he saw Jumba. He knew he
had to get away quickly. If he was
caught, he would be sent to a prison
in space!

Just then Stitch had a great idea . . .

Stitch grabbed Myrtle's trike—
and Lilo's hand. Off they went!
 "Hey! That's my trike!" Myrtle
yelled after them.
 "Bye!" called Lilo.

"Oh, no!" cried Pleakley.
"Stitch is getting away! We've
got to do something!"

Jumba wasn't about to let
Stitch escape.
   "Grab that scooter!" he said.
"We will catch him!"

Lilo and Stitch rode all over the island—up roads, down hills, and around corners. Up ahead, Stitch saw a waterfall. He tried to stop and then . . .
SPLASH!

They got all wet, but Lilo didn't care. Stitch *did* care. He hated water. Lilo didn't realize that they were being chased. But Stitch knew that he and Lilo had to keep moving.

Jumba and Pleakley rode under
the waterfall, too. They got soaked—
and didn't like it one bit.

But the chase was still on!
Jumba called out, "When you are
ready to give up, just let us know!
Ha! Ha!"

Soon Stitch came to a cliff at one end of the island. He knew Jumba and Pleakley were close behind. There was nowhere to go, just lots and lots of water below.

Stitch was trapped!

Stitch was *not* going to give himself up. He waited until Jumba and Pleakley were almost at the edge. Then Stitch quickly turned around and sped the other way.

But Jumba and Pleakley zoomed right off the cliff . . .

. . . and into the water!

"Ahhhh!" screamed Jumba and Pleakley.

Luckily, the pair of aliens landed right on a surfboard!

A little later, Lilo and Stitch
rode through a local market.
"Yum!" said Lilo, looking at
a piece of fruit.

The others had made it from
the beach to the market, too.
"Noooo!" yelled Pleakley as
Jumba drove right through
the stand. But Jumba didn't
care. He wanted Stitch!

Jumba and Pleakley left the market and were gaining on Lilo and Stitch. They rode past a sleeping volcano.

Suddenly the volcano began to
rumble. Smoke started to fill the sky.
"Uh-oh!" said Lilo looking back.
The volcano was waking up! "Go,
Stitch, *GO!*" she cried.

Stitch rode faster and faster as the lava began to flow.

"Ha! Ha! We have him now," Jumba said.

The aliens were getting closer . . .

. . . but so was the lava!

Finally, Jumba and Pleakley gave up and jumped off the scooter. They climbed a tree to escape. Pleakley explained, "I have just determined this situation to be far too hazardous!"

"Bah!" snorted an angry Jumba.
"Good dog!" Lilo cheered. She never noticed the pair left behind her.

Stitch made it to safety!
"That was fun!" cried
Lilo. "Let's do it again!"
An exhausted Stitch just
rolled his eyes.

Enhance the reading experience with follow-up questions to help your child develop reading comprehension and increase his/her awareness of words.

Approach this with a sense of play. Make a game of having your child answer the questions. You do not need to ask all the questions at one time. Let these questions be fun discussions rather than a test. If your child doesn't have instant recall, encourage him/her to look back into the book to "research" the answers. You'll be modeling what good readers do and, at the same time, forging a sharing bond with your child.

1. Whose trike did Stitch take?

2. How did Jumba and Pleakley disguise themselves?

3. Where did Jumba and Pleakley land when they rode off the cliff?

4. What kind of fruit do you like best?

5. What words can you make from the letters in *volcano?*

6. Which alien has four eyes?

Answers: 1. Myrtle's. 2. as a man and a woman tourist. 3. in the water on a surfboard. 4. answers will vary. 5. *possible answers:* can, an, cool, van, on, loon, no, con. 6. Jumba.